ALIEN BABYSITTING ADVENTURES

Printed in the United States of America
First Paperback Edition, May 2020
1 3 5 7 9 10 8 6 4 2
FAC-029261-20094

Library of Congress Control Number: 2019944913

ISBN 978-1-368-05358-7

For more Disney Press fun, visit www.disneybooks.com
Visit DisneyChannel.com

SUSTAINABLE
FORESTRY
INITIATIVE
Certified Chain of Custody
Promoting Sustainable Forestry
www.sfiprogram.org
SFI-01054
The SFI label applies to the text stock

ALIEN BABYSITTING ADVENTURES

Adapted by Carin Davis

Based on the series pilot, by Mike Alber and Gabe Snyder,

and the "Crybaby Duran" episode, by Heather MacGilvray

and Linda Mathious

DISNEP PRESS

Los Angeles • New York

CHAPTER 1

*B*zzzzzzzzz. *Bzzzzzzzzz. Bzzzzzzzz. . . .*

Gabby Duran was not a fan of mornings. Or her new town of Havensburg. So at 7:45 a.m., when her pink alarm clock rudely buzzed her awake, she did what any sensible person would do. She slammed the snooze button . . . with a brick. Sure, there might have been more elegant ways to quiet the clock. But hey, it got the job done. From Gabby's perspective, that was a win.

She curled up under her fuchsia covers. Recently, Gabby had come to believe that mornings were for suckers. As was this lame town. Havensburg had nothing on Miami, where she'd spent all thirteen years of her life living it up. Gabby had pretty much ruled that city. Then, three weeks ago, everything changed. She and her mom, Dina, and her eight year old sister, Olivia, had packed up their belongings and moved to the quiet town of Havensburg. Talk about upheaval. Gabby missed her friends; she missed the beach; she missed doing her thing. Her mom and sis both slid into suburban life without a glitch. In fact, they were thriving there. But Gabby? She slid in like . . . What's the opposite of a smooth operator? Doesn't matter. She slid in like someone who didn't fit in. Her life was over the minute she hit Havensburg. More like Havens-*boring*.

Gabby tugged on her comforter and glanced around her room. She'd tried to put her own spin on her new space. She painted the walls electric blue, then papered them with concert flyers, cute animal prints, and posters from her top five favorite horror films. She'd strung strands of lights from the ceiling and even painted the wall above her bed with a stylized *Gabby D.* Her room looked sick, but there was only so much style her neon LATER HATER sign could bring to this cookie-cutter town.

Gabby laid her head down on her pillow, her long ombré hair splayed messily about. At least she could snooze the day away, so it wouldn't be a total loss.

No sooner had Gabby shut her eyes than her bedroom

door swung wide open. "Morning, sunshine. Up and at 'em," sang her mom, who was dressed in a pale blush sweater, matching blush pants, and a smile that was way too big for the time of day.

"Your morning attitude, it's off-putting," groaned Gabby.

Dina crossed the cluttered room and raised the window shades. Gabby grimaced at the bright light it let in.

"I'm going to need you to watch your sister for a couple hours today, okay?" As a single mom, Dina counted on her older daughter to look out for her younger one.

Gabby gave her mom a major eye roll. *Babysit? Today?* But in truth, it wasn't like she had anything better to do. No one was blowing up her cell to hang out or texting her to join in. She might as well watch Olivia.

Babysitting, Gabby thought. *If you've got a younger sibling, you're gonna get roped into it sooner or later. Fortunately, I pretty much rule at it.*

An hour later, Gabby sat at the kitchen counter wearing a cropped gray hoodie and counting the cash in an envelope clearly marked *Emergency $.*

"Crazy idea," said Olivia, approaching her sister. Clutched in her hands was a colorful homemade spinner. "What if we spent the day making a new chore wheel?" She pushed her glasses up on her nose.

Wearing a crisp white-collared shirt underneath a neat light blue sweater, Olivia didn't look dressed for a Saturday. Did the girl even own a pair of sweatpants? Gabby would have to work on that.

"Liv, I love you, I do," said Gabby, and she meant it. Her sister was the best. "But someone needs to save you from yourself."

As the older sister, Gabby figured, it was her responsibility to help Liv live a little. Show her there was more to life than chore wheels and rule following. With that goal in mind, Gabby fanned out the crisp bills in her manicured hand. "What if, instead, we spent this twenty bucks Mom left us in case of emergency?"

Liv scrunched up her face, looking perplexed. "But this isn't an emergency."

"If we're talking chore wheels, this is as dire as it gets," Gabby said, studying Olivia's blunt bob and severe bangs.

Gabby had so much to teach Liv about the art of loosening up.

> ☻ <

The Duran sisters stood in the Havensburg grocery, staring up at a towering wall of cereal boxes. There were rows and rows of Dax Flax, Treasure Flakes, and, high on the top shelf, way out of reach, the grand prize: Blammo Bombs.

"Um, you're sure we need Sugar-Frosted Blammo Bombs?" asked Olivia. Just the thought of bending the rules made her itchy. There was still time to turn around.

"The fact that you even have to ask that tells me that we do," said Gabby. Spending the crisis cash on sugar cereal was the plan of a super genius, if she must say so herself.

"Get climbin'," she instructed with a flick of her hand. For a girl in camo shorts and a bucket hat, she sounded pretty authoritative.

Liv started to scale the cereal wall. "Um, these shelves don't feel super sturdy." She looked down; the ground seemed really, really far away. "Are you even watching me?" she asked Gabby.

"Of course I am," said Gabby, not bothering to look up from the box label she was studying. Who knew cereal contained so much riboflavin? Fascinating.

Olivia stretched out her arm as far as she could to grab the Blammo Bombs with the tips of her fingers. But suddenly, the shelf beneath her feet collapsed and she tumbled to the ground with a thud, buried beneath an avalanche of Dax Flax and Treasure Flakes.

Gabby looked up. Huh, who would have thought the shelves weren't sturdy? She learned something new every day.

> ● <

Gabby opened the front door to the Duran house with one hand and held a bag of frozen peas to Olivia's head with the other. She was not about to let this minor cereal incident slow the Duran girls' roll. She checked Liv's head for bumps and bruises. "Well, there's no swelling, so that's good. You sure you're okay?"

"I'm fine," Liv said, smiling. "Plus, how could I be mad? You introduced me to these guys." She hugged a box of Blammo Bombs to her chest. Olivia shoved a fistful of cereal into her mouth and scampered off to read a book.

See? Babysitting's a piece of cake, thought Gabby. The key to being a stellar babysitter wasn't staying clear of trouble; it was untangling the trouble before the parents came home.

CHAPTER 2

*T*he next morning, the Duran sisters sat side by side eating breakfast at the kitchen island. Gabby threw back a couple of breakfast taquitos while scrolling through social media. Her old Miami friends' feeds were filled with beach selfies and sunlit smiles.

"Aw, Katrina and Michelle. I miss those girls," said Dina, peering over Gabby's shoulder. "You should call them. There's no reason you girls can't be friends."

"Mom, it's been three weeks and we moved eight states away. They've already moved on," said Gabby. She stared at an image of three girls cracking up. What she wouldn't give to be one of them.

"They have not moved on," insisted Dina.

"They've already replaced me. You see this girl? I don't

know this girl." She held up the phone for her mom to see. "Say hello to Gabby 2.0. The new me."

Gabby swiped through picture after picture of Katrina and Michelle with the mystery girl. The fact that they'd filled her spot so quickly stung. "Can we just move back to Miami?" Gabby asked.

Dina smoothed her black dress; her hair and makeup were camera ready. "Gabby, I know this has been hard for you. But it is what's best for the family. I mean, the school district here has a gifted program that can challenge Olivia in ways her old school just couldn't."

Gabby didn't understand why her social life had to suffer just because her sister was some kind of brainiac.

"And Mom was offered an on-air position for Local 6. How could she pass that up?" chimed in Olivia.

"Maybe this will cheer you up: I'm on mugs now!" Dina held up a Local 6 News Team mug with her face on it.

"Mugs, Gabby!" said Olivia, bursting with excitement.

Gabby stared at the coffee cup and her face broke into a giant smile. "Wow, that does actually make me feel better."

"Really?" Dina smiled.

"Nope," Gabby said emphatically. Look, she was thrilled about her mom's success; she'd worked tirelessly to rock her career. But that didn't change how Gabby felt about Havensburg. It was the pits.

"I'm glad you two have a new job and a new school. But what do I have here?" asked Gabby. She already knew the answer to her question. She had nothing. Nada. Blank emoji.

Dina hated to see her daughter rattled. "You're gonna find something, Gabby. I know you," she said with an encouraging nod.

Gabby stood, not all that cheered up, and grabbed a handful of taquitos for the road. She had to get to school. Because nothing said fun like a day at Havensburg Junior High.

CHAPTER 3

*G*abby stood in the crowded school hallway and surveyed the scene. Groups of cheerful students chatted away at their lockers. They chuckled at private jokes she wasn't in on and rehashed weekend memories she wasn't a part of.

Her eyes darted from student to student until they fell on Wesley. Wesley, a kindhearted kid who wore his weirdness with pride, was the president of the Mysteries of Havensburg Club. He was tall for his age, and his mussed-up auburn hair gave him another two inches of height. He'd always been fascinated by the idea that there was more to life than met the eye. At that moment, he was attempting to enlist new members to his cause. "Join the Mysteries of Havensburg Club!" he called out, waving a pamphlet in his hand.

Gabby noted that Wesley's recruitment skills left something to be desired. He solicited every kid who walked by. And every kid ignored him.

Wes shouted, undeterred. Still, he couldn't help feeling perplexed. Had those people no sense of curiosity? Didn't they ponder the existence of paranormal forces at work right there in Havensburg? There had to be one other person who thought the town was messed up.

That was when he noticed Gabby standing alone in the hallway. With her gold sneaks and black floral backpack, the new girl looked like someone who believed in conspiracy theories. Or at least someone who wasn't afraid to think her own thing.

"Gabby," he said, pointing at her. "Care to sign up for the Mysteries of Havensburg Club?"

Unlike the others, Gabby didn't scurry away. She walked toward him.

Wes smiled; he'd never gotten that far in a conversation with a potential recruit. "We investigate weird and potentially paranormal occurrences around town. You know, ghosts, Bigfoot . . . Dobek the janitor. I think he's been collecting student garbage."

Wes side-nodded toward a completely unsuspicious-looking gentleman in a green uniform at the end of the hall. "I have no idea why, but I'm pretty sure the reason is paranormal-slash-supernatural in nature," he whispered. "I'd bring my trash home with me if I were you."

Gabby's eyes traveled to Wes's unzipped duffel, which was overstuffed with crumpled papers and orange peels.

"So, you interested in signing up? We could use a second member," Wesley said in a singsong.

Gabby considered him. Wes's obsession with Dobek was weird, but his commitment to the theory was impressive. He looked so hopeful standing there, with his cute eye-inside-a-pyramid T-shirt. Plus, Gabby liked that Wes wasn't afraid to be different. He gave off an "I'm here, and I believe in ridiculous nonsense, so deal with it" attitude that Gabby could respect.

"Eh, it weirdly does sound kinda fun," admitted Gabby. And if she was planning to stick around Havensburg, she might consider joining. "But I don't think I'm gonna be in this town much longer."

As if on cue, the school PA system clicked to life and

a loud voice boomed over it: "Gabby Duran to the office. Now."

Gabby's face lit up with happiness. "I'm getting kicked out of school," she said.

Gabby had never done anything in Miami that caused her to be called to the principal's office. But desperate times called for bold measures, which was how she found herself seated across from Havensburg Junior High's own Principal Swift. The peculiar man was dressed like an over-layered professor, in a suit jacket, an argyle sweater-vest, a button-down collared shirt, and a bow tie. Swift seemed fidgety and awkward in his own skin, but Gabby chalked that up to the fact that he was British.

Gabby took in her surroundings; so *that* was what a principal's office looked like. She was expecting something less generic. The dusty books that lined the shelves seemed like they'd never been cracked. A strange tin labeled *Just Normal Mints* took center stage on his desk next to a Newton's cradle. She studied his vintage engraved name plaque and wondered why he bothered. How many students sat across from him and didn't know his name?

Gabby was going to go with a guess of zero. *Way to pick a super-lame desk trinket, Principal Swift.*

After several tense moments, Swift cleared his throat and popped a Just Normal Mint into his mouth. His whole face contorted as he sucked on it, as if he wasn't used to eating hard candies. He stared down at Gabby and began to speak. "*Ahem.* A curious thing happened as I stepped out to my automobile today. My car had been mummified in duct tape and tagged with graffiti."

Swift continued. "It said 'Gabby Duran did this' with your student ID.

"So tell me, Gabby, was the sprayed paint correct?" he asked, his eyes narrowing in inquisition. "Did you indeed cover my automobile in duct tape?"

"Yup. You caught me. It was me," said Gabby, eager to claim responsibility. Her grand plan was working flawlessly.

"Then I suppose I need to thank you," said Swift, almost giddy.

Gabby sat up straight with confusion. Guy in the bow tie said what? She'd vandalized his car. He was supposed to expel her, not thank her.

"Clearly you were just trying to protect it from falling

bird excrement," gushed Swift. "And I must say, I under-stand the impulse. I, too, despise all these birds and their freewheeling, excrete-as-you-may lifestyle. It's an affront to civilized people everywhere. So thank you, Gabby, for helping your fellow man."

Gabby panicked. How had her plan gone so awry? She was miffed. "So, am I getting kicked out of school, or what?" she asked, hoping to get back to the discipline at hand.

"I should think not," he said, laughing.

That was not the answer Gabby was looking for. "Okay, then," she said, speaking slowly. "I want you to remember that you left me no choice."

Without warning, Gabby frantically swept her arms across Principal Swift's desk, sending his knickknacks and papers flying. In a fit of rage, she overturned office chairs, tossed his books in the air, and trashed the principal's office to pieces. His *Principal Swift* nameplate didn't stand a chance.

CHAPTER 4

*T*he sun shone brightly through the living room window, but at the moment, Dina Duran did not have a sunny disposition. In fact, she was exasperated.

"What were you thinking?" she scolded Gabby. "He could have kicked you out of school." Dina was shocked when she'd received the phone call from Gabby's school. She had raised her daughter to be better than that, to show respect for authority and to always carry herself with grace.

Gabby started to defend herself. "Yeah, but, Mom, I—"

Dina cut off her daughter with a steely glance and a single raised eyebrow. Olivia, who sat watching the argument, looked discontent, as well. She expected more of her older sister.

"I know. I know. I went too far this time," Gabby admitted.

"You duct-taped the man's car!" said Dina, raising both eyebrows.

Gabby couldn't bear to look her disappointed mom in the eye. So instead she glanced around the room, with its lush turquoise couch and mod yellow chairs. "I just . . . I want to go back to my old life," Gabby confessed. There, she'd said it. Maybe now everything could return to the way it was.

"Gabby, this is your life now. You have to try and make the best of it." Dina gestured to the mantel; it was overcrowded with Olivia's academic trophies and Dina's reporting awards. "Look at your sister: she was just named Student of the Month at her school." Dina pointed toward a newly framed certificate.

"Student of the Month?" Gabby said, turning toward Olivia. "We've only been here three weeks!"

Her precocious sister shrugged. "What can I say? It's been a whirlwind."

"Okay, well, we need to get in front of this," Dina announced, shifting into solution gear. "You and I are going over to Principal Swift's house to apologize."

"Going over to his house?" Gabby's long hair swayed

as she shook her head. Her mom clearly didn't understand how much the kids at school would laugh if they found out she'd visited Swift at home. And they already didn't like her. "Look, Mom, I know I stepped over the line this time. But how about I just do it at school tomorrow?"

"I don't know that you *will* do it at school tomorrow, Gabby," Dina said, her voice sounding like a newscaster's even when she wasn't on TV. "I mean, you're trashing principals' offices now? Who knows what you're gonna do?"

Gabby was hurt. Her mom had never lost faith in her before. She had to fix this. "Okay, fine. I'll go apologize. But I'm gonna do it on my own so I can prove to you I'm a responsible, trustworthy person."

Dina's skeptical expression softened into a smile. That was the considerate daughter she knew and loved.

"Oh, Gabby, wait," she called out, remembering something. "Bring him one of these." Dina handed her daughter a Local 6 News Team mug with her face on it. "What? People love mugs."

Gabby shrugged and reluctantly headed out on her errand.

⌐ ⋊ ⊤ △ ⋎ ⬓ ⚬ ⎖ ⁒ ⬜

CHAPTER 5

*P*rincipal *Swift* didn't *live* far *from* Gabby. *She* shifted the Local 6 News Team mug in her hand as she walked up Swift's front steps and rang the bell. No answer. "Hello?" She tugged on the door; it was locked.

Gabby surveyed her surroundings while waiting for an answer. The house was big and brown and eerily quiet. She muttered to herself, "Way to pick a super-creepy house, guy."

Gabby decided to take matters into her own hands. She crossed the front porch, turned down the side path, and knocked on the back door. "Hello? Anybody? I am one hundred percent not coming back here again," she yelled to no one in particular.

Lifting herself up on her tippy-toes, Gabby peered through the back door blinds. There was no movement inside. "Well, I guess this was all just one big waste of—"

Gabby spun around to find herself face to face with a seven-foot-tall . . . um . . . well . . . she wasn't even sure what to call that thing. A giant slimy blob monster? A green goo beast? Whatever it was, it opened its gaping jaw to reveal rows of sharpened teeth.

"*Graraaaaaahhhhh!*" roared the blob monster, its gargantuan tongue flapping about.

"*Aaaaaagggghhhhh!*" Gabby roared right back.

The ginormous blob towered over Gabby's petite frame. But did she run away? Please. Gabby Duran? As if! She grabbed a rake off the ground, brandished it like a sword, and attacked the beast head-on.

"Aaggghh! Get away from me, you gross whatever you are!" she shouted, walloping the blob again and again with the rake. She'd show him. No one crept up on Gabby Duran and got away with it.

"Time-out! Time-out! Time-out!" called the blob, suddenly morphing into a small eight-year-old boy with tousled brown hair. Dressed in a green striped tee and jeans he'd rolled up at the ankles, the boy looked like an average elementary school student. His name was Jeremy. He tried to shield himself from Gabby's blows. "Time-out!"

Upholding the universal playground rule, Gabby acquiesced and lowered the rake. Her brain couldn't process what she'd just seen. On a scale of one to weird, it was off-the-charts bizarre. "Seriously, what is going—"

Before Gabby could finish that thought, she was zapped unconscious by an otherworldly device.

When Gabby came to, she was clamped into a futuristic silver chair in an egg-shaped room. The black-and-white walls glowed with pulsing light, and a complex communication console sat to her right. A menacing metal orb floated above her.

"Consciousness detected," said the Orb in a stilted, robotic voice. "State your name."

Gabby stared at the Orb incredulously. "State my name? State your name!" Clearly the over-entitled soccer ball didn't know whom he was dealing with. "I have rights, you know. You can't—"

"Subject hostile," declared the Orb. Its surface lights started to flash in a threatening manner. "Begin probing sequence." A laser-edged scalpel extended from the sphere and advanced toward Gabby's head.

She pulled against the arm restraints, but they were too tight. They wouldn't budge. "Hey! Don't you get any closer. . . . I, uh, took two years of karate!" threatened Gabby, refusing to show fear.

The Orb considered the strange human in front of it, then cut the distance between them. "Probability assessment: Subject is lying."

"You're right," Gabby said, smirking. "It was two years of youth soccer! And I hated it!" In a whirl of motion, Gabby threw back her body with all the force she could muster. She tipped the chair back and bicycle-kicked the Orb straight across the room. Freaky robot or not, no one messed with Gabby Duran.

With the chair knocked over, Gabby was able to free herself from the arm restraints and rushed full speed for the door. Freedom was a few feet away. But just before she reached the entrance, the strangest thing happened: a houseplant positioned next to the door morphed into Principal Swift.

Whoa, whoa, whoa, wait—what? Now she'd seen it all. "Principal Swift?" Gabby asked, gaping. "What is going on?" She backed up, ready to take a flying leap at him if necessary.

"Come, Gabby. There is much to discuss."

Come? With him? Just your average, run-of-the-mill houseplant–slash–school administrator? "Okay, first item to discuss," challenged Gabby. "Where are we?"

Swift pressed a button. The metallic door slid open with a futuristic purr to reveal the bottom few steps of a very ordinary staircase. Stacked to the side were old cardboard boxes labeled *Halloween Decorations*, *Christmas Lights*, and *To Donate*.

"My basement," answered Swift as if that had been obvious all along.

ⴺ ⚔ ⊤ △ ✕ ⴺ ≗ ⅁ ⁒ ⌀

CHAPTER 6

Gabby followed Principal Swift up the staircase and into his living room. Compared with the cutting-edge communications room below, the decor looked like something someone's great-uncle left them. Tufted leather couches, old-fashioned lamps, and dark wood bookcases filled the space. A phrenology bust sat atop a stodgy coffee table.

Gabby plopped down on the couch next to Swift, still trying to process everything she'd just seen. Blob monsters, alien tech, and now the strangest thing of all: a massive tray of shrimp cocktail set out on Swift's coffee table. Swift was eating shrimp after shrimp, tails and all. Jeremy kept flicking shrimp into the air, trying to catch it in his mouth and failing horribly. This was so not normal.

"Ooooooh, yummy," said Swift, licking his fingers.

Gabby had to ask. "So you two are—"

"Aliens, yes," confirmed Swift. "Jeremy and I are Gor-Mons—shape-shifters from the planet Gor-Monia," he explained, as if that was a planet Gabby had heard of. It was not. But she wasn't sure if that was because it wasn't part of this solar system or because she'd zoned out in astronomy class. It was honestly a toss-up.

"Shrimp cocktail?" offered Swift. "I'm told it's a very popular human meal."

Gabby lifted a shrimp off the tray. The shellfish was rubbery, overcooked, and utterly unappealing. She was definitely not going to eat it. "I'm good, thanks," she said, dropping the shrimp back onto the tray. "Also, I don't think you're supposed to eat the tails."

"Oh, um, oh . . . ahhh," said Swift, pulling several shrimp tails from his mouth. "Well, when in Rome . . ." He placed the tails in his front shirt pocket. Gabby gave up on correcting him. Instead, she leaned in and tried to focus on Swift's words.

"Jeremy is heir to the Gor-Monite throne," continued

Swift. "However, there are some on our planet who would be less than happy to see him rise to the position of supreme leader."

"You get in my mouth, shrimp," ordered Jeremy, tossing yet another shrimp in the air.

Gabby watched as that shrimp, too, bounced off the future leader's forehead. "Really? That kid?" she quipped. "Can't imagine why. . . ." His food-catching game was not on point.

"Yes, well, as his uncle, it is my job to keep him hidden here, in the most boring Earth town we could find, until he comes of age. Obviously, keeping our alien identities a secret is of the utmost importance. However, Jeremy has certain behavioral challenges that can complicate things."

They both observed the boy, who was still struggling with the shrimp. "Stupid thing's broken!" whined Jeremy, throwing the crustacean to the ground in frustration. "I'm calling the police," he said, and picked up his cell.

"Stop that!" Swift slapped the phone away from the boy. Had the child no common sense? He turned his attention back to Gabby. "My job at the school helps us blend in seamlessly to Earth culture." His face contorted into an unearthly expression, and he started to violently clear something from his throat. "*Ach, chhhaaaaa.* Sorry. Shrimp tails." He pulled one from his mouth.

Gabby was just glad he hadn't decided to try lobster.

Swift carried on. "But what it also means is that I can't watch him all the time. Now, as such, I require a good babysitter. That's where you come in," he said, finally arriving at his point.

"Whoa, whoa, hold up." Gabby held up her hand and looked at Swift. He had to be joking. "Babysitting? That's what this is about? Sorry to say it, but you got the wrong kid, Swifty." She turned to stand up, hoping she could still make it home in time for her mom's enchilada casserole. It was Wednesday, after all.

Swift looked Gabby in the eye, his face expressing nothing but the highest respect for her. "Oh, Gabby, Gabby, Gabby, Gabby, Gabby, Gabby, Gabby. I have precisely the right kid. You may be the most fearless, resourceful human I have ever met. The way you handled yourself in the basement. The way you attacked Jeremy when he revealed his true, admittedly hideous self. The way you nobly shielded my car from the droppings of those foul, vile birds."

Gabby jumped in. "Again, that's really not—"

Swift held up his finger to stop her midsentence. "Gabbity, Gab, Gab. There's something special about you, Gabby. If anyone on Earth can babysit Jeremy, you can," he said, pointing right at her.

Gabby let his words bounce about her brain. Special? Fearless? Noble? A smile crept across her face. Maybe this weird alien dude actually got her after all. Finally, someone in Havensburg who could see her for who she was.

"Wait! You want her to babysit me?" questioned Jeremy, offended by the very suggestion.

Gabby noticed the boy's movements were jerky and awkward, as if he wasn't quite comfortable in his own skin . . . which suddenly made sense. It was all starting to come together.

"Yes, Jeremy. That's literally what we've been talking about this entire time," said Swift, reaching his breaking point with his nephew.

"No way! Humans are gross," announced Jeremy. "And that one smells like taquitos."

"Hey, taquitos are awesome! You're gross!" Okay, it

was admittedly not Gabby's best comeback, but she wasn't about to let anyone—or any alien—insult the greatest food in the galaxy.

"You're gross!" shouted Jeremy.

"Jeremy, why don't you go help yourself to an ice cream sandwich from the freezer?" suggested Swift.

"Free ice cream sandwich? Baller," said Jeremy, trying out what he thought was a commonly used Earthling expression. "But this isn't over, human. You and me are now serious frenemies." He gave Gabby the stink eye as he morphed back into his gelatinous blob form. Then he oozed out of the room, making an odd squishing sound.

Swift turned to Gabby. "So what do you say?"

Gabby responded without hesitation. "Yeah . . . I'm in!" It was all so weird . . . and so incredibly awesome.

CHAPTER 7

*T*he next day, Gabby strutted down the school hall-way in white flowered shorts, a cropped goldenrod jacket, and matching goldenrod high-tops. She had a new bounce in her step. She'd gotten her groove back, plus some. Maybe Havensburg wasn't so loathsome after all. She, the one and only Gabby Duran, had been tapped by Principal Swift to babysit aliens. It didn't get more dope than that.

She spotted Wesley at his locker. "Wesley!" she shouted, saluting her friend. *Friend*—Gabby liked the sound of that.

"Oh, hey! Look who didn't get kicked out of school!" Wesley replied.

"Yep. I guess I'm here to stay," said Gabby, realizing she was actually happy about that. "Speaking of which, does that club of yours ever talk about, like . . . aliens?"

Wesley's face lit up. "Um, only all the time. I've never actually been able to prove alien existence in Havensburg, though. If they are here, they are super good at blending in."

Gabby smiled to herself. If Wes had seen Swift and Jeremy attempting to eat shrimp, he'd revise that statement.

Wes looked at Gabby, his eyes filled with optimism. "So does this mean you wanna join?"

"Sure," said Gabby cheerfully. "Why not?"

"Wait, really?" he said with a giant grin, hardly able to control his excitement.

"Yeah. You seem cool." Gabby gave his arm a little punch. "And I'm starting to feel like this club is really something I should be a part of."

"Yes! You are not gonna regret this!" Wesley cheered. He wrapped Gabby in a huge bear hug.

Gabby reported to Principal Swift's house directly after school. Getting to babysit an alien was basically the most exciting thing that had ever happened to her, and she didn't want to be late. Standing in Swift's living room, she riffled through some magazines, then held up a piece of his mail. It was addressed to Mr. Principal Swift. *Huh . . .*

"'Mr. Principal Swift,'" Gabby read aloud. She wanted to make sure she was seeing that correctly. "So your first name is just Principal?" She gawked, eyebrows raised.

"Yes," said Swift, as if stating the obvious.

"Your name is just Principal Swift?" Gabby asked again.

"Yes, Gabby. Obviously. How else would people know that I'm a principal?" Swift grabbed a file folder that had been sitting on a leather chair. He couldn't understand where this silly question was going. He'd selected an appropriate Earthling alias that clearly identified his profession. What was the issue?

"So you go to a dentist, and he says—"

"Gabby, please! We need to finish going through the rules." He tucked the file into his briefcase and clipped it shut. "Rule number seventy-four: Absolutely no soda pop of any sort."

Gabby glanced down at her tote bag, which was crammed with two-liter soda bottles and boxes of frozen taquitos. They were the two key ingredients in her secret recipe for a highly successful babysitting session. "No soda? Why not?"

Principal Swift glanced at her dubiously. "That was covered extensively in the orientation materials I gave you. Now, you did read the orientation materials I gave you?"

If by "read," Principal Principal Swift meant "dumped them in the kitchen trash without bothering to look at them," then . . . "Of course. I mean, who doesn't love long, boring binders of instructions?"

"Exactly!" said Swift, pleased to find someone who loved rules as much as he did.

"Now, I'm holding a mandatory safety seminar for the teachers and I should be back in a couple of hours," said Swift. "Oh, and you'll need this." He pulled an outdated razor-style flip phone from his pocket and gave it to her.

Gabby stared at the hinged device in her hand. She was pretty sure her abuela had the same one. "Cool. One super-old phone," she said smugly.

"No. One incredibly powerful piece of alien technology to aid in your babysitting duties," Swift corrected her. "As you can see, I've disguised it to seamlessly blend in with Earth culture."

That was true, if they were talking about Earth culture circa 2004. Gabby flipped open the phone and a high-tech alien interface sprang to life. The glowing symbols and bleeping configurations were like nothing Gabby had ever encountered. Was she supposed to tap them or swipe them? Did this thing have a data plan? Could she text Mars?

"I won't waste time explaining how to use it," noted Swift, "since that was also covered extensively in the orientation materials. Now, if you'll excuse me . . ." He walked with purpose toward the front door.

Ugh, again with the orientation materials. Rule book, schmule book. Gabby's babysitting game was on point. Did she really need to waste her time sifting through an encyclopedia of orientation materials?

With Swift's back still to her, Gabby eagerly thumbed at random symbols on the flip phone's interface. A potent pulse of blue energy rushed out from the phone and rippled across the room, where it disintegrated an expensive-looking vase. Gabby was startled. Maybe she shouldn't have pushed the button without reading the instructions. Oh well, too late. She desperately jabbed at the phone's interface again. Didn't the thing have a reverse button? Before she could locate one, she heard Swift say, "Gabby . . ."

He turned around to look at her intensely. "You are now responsible for the future leader of an entire planet. I'm placing a lot of trust in you," he said.

Gabby flashed her megawatt smile. "Swifty, come on! I got this. Everything is gonna be fine," she assured him, shifting her weight from one foot to the other in an attempt to block Swift's view of the empty spot formerly occupied by a valuable vase.

Swift gave Gabby a curt nod good-bye, then left the future of Gor-Monia under her responsible watch.

As soon as Swift shut the door, Gabby reached for her secret stash of soda and taquitos. If Jeremy was going to learn to blend in with Earth culture, he might as well start by learning to eat like a human.

> 👽 <

A dozen spicy taquitos and three two-liter bottles of root beer later, Gabby and Jeremy were having a blast. Gabby was thoroughly impressed by how quickly the alien kid adopted the sloth-like qualities of an Earthling tween. He was splayed out on the couch, not a care in the galaxy.

"*Buuuuuuuurp.* You were right," Jeremy said after a huge swig of soda. "Taquitos rule." He chugged the rest of the bottle, then tossed it aside with attitude.

"I told ya, kid. I got mad wisdom," said Gabby, tapping away at random buttons on the alien flip phone. To her surprise, the phone projected a 3-D hologram of the universe. It twinkled and rotated and emitted a slightly tinny sound.

"Whoa," said Gabby, stunned. There was so much to learn about alien life. She could not wait.

Jeremy tossed a taquito in the air and tried to catch it in his mouth. The taquito ricocheted off his face and into his lap. He threw it toward his mouth again. This time, the taquito flew over the back of the couch he was lounging on.

Gabby chuckled. He'd master it eventually. In the meantime, she had about a zillion questions for the Gor-Monite kid. She started with the most obvious. "So what's up with your shape-shifting, huh? Can you just change into whatever you want?" she asked, tucking her straight brown hair behind her ears.

"I wish," Jeremy said dreamily. "Gor-Mons are digestive

shape-shifters, which means I can only change into things I eat."

Gabby stared at Jeremy's pint-sized human form. "So . . . you, like, ate a kid?"

"The hair of one," said Jeremy with pride.

"Cool, cool," said Gabby, a little grossed out and a lot fascinated. She keyed another arbitrary sequence into Swift's fancy phone and the hologram disappeared.

Jeremy eyed the flip phone with envy. "I can't believe Principal let you use that. He never lets me do anything, because he thinks I'll mess up and let everyone know we're aliens. You know, I've never even been bowling. Or to the movies. Or a drive-through."

Gabby gasped at the injustice. What kind of cruel alien species didn't believe in the greatest human invention ever? "Seriously? You've never been to a drive-through? That's messed up, man. Drive-throughs rule."

"I bet they do!" Jeremy kicked one foot against the other, frustrated. He knew this stupid planet had a lot more to offer than just this dumb old house. If only his lame uncle would let him get out and explore it. "Sometimes I wish he trusted me more, you know."

Gabby felt for the kid. "Yeah, I know how that goes. My mom doesn't really trust me, either. Even though I'm pretty much the most responsible person I know."

Just then, a disturbingly loud gurgling sound interrupted their conversation. It was coming from Jeremy's human-form stomach. He pulled aside his navy button-down shirt and slowly lifted his striped tee. His stomach was bubbling and rolling in an unnatural way. He was almost 100 percent positive his Earthling body wasn't supposed to be doing that. "Um . . ." He looked at Gabby quizzically. "What's happening to me?" His voice trembled slightly with fear.

"Probably nothing," said Gabby, who was freaking out a little on the inside. Jeremy's stomach was sloshing and churning in a grotesque way. "But still . . ." She grabbed her personal cell and quickly dialed Principal Principal.

He picked up immediately. "Yes, Gabby . . . ?" She'd caught Swift in the middle of explaining CPR to the teachers.

"Hey, Swifty, quick question." Gabby did her best to sound casual and nonchalant, as if what she was about to ask was no biggie. "Hypothetically, if Jeremy's stomach was, like, uh, bubbling a little, what would that be all about?"

Jeremy's stomach grumbled and snarled loudly, as if he'd eaten a monster.

"Well, Jeremy assimilates the molecular structure of anything he ingests," explained Swift. "So if you gave him soda pop, for example, it would mean that his body had absorbed the volatile, carbonated qualities of the drink, effectively turning him into a time bomb that would explode in approximately one hour, destroying him and anything else within a hundred-foot radius. But you definitely did not give him soda pop, correct?"

Gabby eyed the empty root beer bottles that littered the couch. Jeremy had guzzled down four of them. "You think I'd do something that irresponsible?" Gabby guffawed. "Honestly, it's like you don't even know me at all."

"Very well, then. I have to go. Bye-bye," said Swift, returning to his safety seminar.

Gabby was mortified as she turned to face Jeremy. She had no clue how to break the news to him gently. "So," she said, waving her hands around nervously, "don't make a whole big thing of it, but it looks like you're gonna blow up."

Jeremy sprang from the couch. His panicked little face said it all. He did not want to explode.

CHAPTER 8

*G*abby and Jeremy rushed into the Duran house and beelined for the kitchen trash can. "Okay, no need to panic," said Gabby as she frantically dumped the garbage can out on the floor. "We've got like"—she did the math in her head—"forty-seven minutes to figure this out."

Gabby reminded herself to breathe. She was the indomitable Gabby Duran; she could do this. She sifted through food-soaked takeout containers, used tissues, and wrappers.

Jeremy watched her with concern. "I'm gonna be okay, though, right, Gabby? I mean, after I blow up?"

"Um . . . yeah, sure. Why not?" Gabby knew nothing about Gor-Monite biology, but she was pretty sure self-explosion was bad no matter what planet you hailed from.

"Bingo! Orientation materials!" she yelled, picking up a thick binder. Gabby flipped open the binder and began to read through the pages with speed. She came to a stop on a chapter titled "So Your Gor-Mon Child Is Going to Blow Up."

Yup, that pretty much summed up her current situation. She scanned the page, zooming past the part with scientific diagrams of molecules that might as well have been written in Alien. Finally, she spotted a paragraph in English.

"Okay, here we go . . ." she said, then read aloud: " 'To prevent explosion, feed your child sodium silicate—a mineral found in the soil of Zzzansar VII, some polydimensional light beings, and Gor-Monite breath mints." She slammed the binder shut with satisfaction. She had this!

"That's it! Swift's always popping those weird mints!" Boom. Problem solved.

Jeremy was beyond relieved. "Baller! I'll just call him and—"

Gabby batted Jeremy's phone out of his hands. "No way, you doof! He cannot find out about this."

Jeremy crinkled his forehead. "Wait. I thought we didn't want me to blow up?"

Gabby glared at Jeremy. Did she have to spell it out for the kid? Then she remembered Jeremy wasn't a kid, or at least not a human one. She took a patient breath and explained. "Jeremy, do you see that mantel over there?" She nodded toward the fireplace shelf, which was lined with Dina's and Olivia's accolades and awards. "My whole life, my mom and sister have been doing these great things and getting all these awards. But me? I've always just been the family screwup."

She looked at Jeremy and got real. "This babysitting job is my chance to do something great, too. Principal Swift is trusting me with one of the most important jobs in the galaxy, and I am not about to make him think I can't do it.

"Now let's do the responsible thing and go steal some breath mints," she proposed.

Gabby and Jeremy crouched outside the double doors of the school cafeteria, watching Swift's in-progress safety seminar. The best Gabby could tell, Swift was attempting to teach the faculty about the Heimlich maneuver. He held a CPR dummy and with every movement yelled, "Abdominal thrust, abdominal thrust!"

Gabby gazed past Swift at his suit jacket, which was slung over the back of a chair a few feet behind him. In its pocket was the coveted Gor-Monite breath mint tin. Target acquired.

"Now," Swift continued, looking down at the dummy, which wore a T-shirt and a baseball cap, "it's always important to wear a hat."

Gabby didn't want to hurt Swifty's feelings or anything, but she was pretty sure that wasn't how the Heimlich worked. But no time for that lesson. She had an explosion to stop. And based on the cacophony coming from Jeremy's stomach, she assumed her time was running out.

"You sure about this?" asked Jeremy. His stomach growled and roiled.

"No, you're right. Let's just go home and let you explode," said Gabby, straight-faced. What did she have to do to earn a little faith around here? "C'mon, trust me! I'm a wizard." She had everything under control.

Just then, she heard someone say, "Gabby?"

She spun around. Standing right behind them was Wesley. Gabby did her best to act natural. "Oh. Hi, Wesley. What, uh, what are you doing here, after school?"

Wesley leaned in, just in case anyone else was listening. "Well, I left some trash in my locker and I gotta get to it before Dobek does, because my DNA is all over that stuff."

Gabby nodded. She should have guessed it was something like that.

Wesley paused for a moment. "What are you doing here?"

"Me? I, uh . . ." Gabby searched for a logical explanation.

"We're here to steal my uncle's breath mints so I don't explode," Jeremy offered all matter-of-factly. The future leader of Gor-Monia stuck out his hand toward Wesley and introduced himself. "I'm Jeremy, by the way. I'm an ali—"

A powerful pulse of energy rippled through Wesley, causing him to collapse in a heap.

"Sorry, bud," said Gabby. She held Swift's alien flip phone open in her hand. "Couldn't let you hear that last part." Gabby felt a little bad about zapping her only friend, but she took solace in the fact that Wesley would have loved nothing more than to know that not only did alien technology exist but he'd been zapped by it. She reasoned it would pretty much be the best day of his life.

Jeremy's stomach rumbled and rolled, reminding Gabby she couldn't worry about Wes right then. The solution to all their problems lay just on the other side of the cafeteria door. She needed a plan.

"We just need a distraction so we can get those min—" Something in the school's trophy case caught Gabby's attention. Among the soccer championship cups and badminton participation plaques sat the school mascot, a taxidermic condor. Gabby eyed the animal and smiled; she was having an aha moment.

"How would you feel about eating some dead bird?" she asked Jeremy.

Nobody did distractions like Gabby Duran.

A few minutes later, Swift stood at the front of the cafeteria, heading toward the grand finale of his staff safety seminar. "And one more abdominal thrust!" Swift pronounced. With that, he tossed the first-aid dummy to the floor and clapped his hands together. "Now, that brings us to our next issue: my automobile is currently covered in duct tape. Can anyone give me a ride home?"

None of the staff members volunteered.

Just then, Jeremy, having taken the form of a condor, burst into the room with his wings flapping. He squawked, then dive-bombed the staff, who scattered in panic. Swift, however, didn't run. He held his head high and stood his ground against the unwelcome creature.

"Aha! I told you this day would come!" Swift yelled to his staff. Just as he'd predicted, the birds of the planet had come to attack. "Couldn't defile my vehicle, so you came for me instead, eh, bird? Well, come at me! Now, no one panic! I will establish dominance."

Swift raised his hands and beckoned the bird forth. Then he broke into what Gabby could only describe as a gawky peacock strut. Swift flapped his arms about in a fit. He jerked his neck back and forth in an ungainly fashion and paraded around the room making *koo-kaw* sounds. She'd never seen anyone fully commit to birdcalling like that. It was weirdly impressive.

"*Koo-kaw.* I'm the boss. I'm the boss here," Swift shrieked at condor Jeremy, his arms thrashing about.

With Swift fully distracted by his bird dance, Gabby darted for his suit jacket and searched his pockets. Yes, she found it! She grabbed the tin of mints, gave condor Jeremy a thumbs-up, then took off for the music room, where she and Jeremy had agreed to meet.

In the classroom, Gabby paced among the cellos and drum sets and stared at the clock. They had just enough time for Jeremy to eat a mint before he went *ka-blam*. If he didn't show up soon, her plan would be toast.

Finally, Jeremy rushed in, huffing and puffing.

"It's about time," said Gabby.

"Sorry, that guy really hates birds," he said, trying to catch his breath. Gabby couldn't argue with that.

"You get the mints?" he asked.

"Right here," said Gabby, holding up the tin with relief.

Gabby and Jeremy leaned over the tin as she opened it, then both immediately stood up in shock. *What? No!* It couldn't be.

"Empty," gasped Gabby.

Jeremy stared at the bare tin in disbelief. Swift had popped every last Gor-Monite mint. Their plan had failed. "No mints. I'm gonna blow up," he said, slumping into a blue plastic chair. His stomach grumbled in confirmation. Jeremy glowered at Gabby. "You know, I'm starting to think you might not be a very good babysitter."

Alien said what? Nobody called Gabby Duran a bad babysitter. She flashed her signature smile. Was it time to panic yet? Nope, not in a million light-years. "No, I'm a great babysitter. And we've still got one more shot."

Gabby grabbed Jeremy's hand and sprinted down the hall with him. All fury and fire, they burst into the cafeteria, where Swift was still straightening up from the recent condor attack.

"Hey, Swifty!" she yelled, not bothering to slow down. Her eyes zeroed in on Principal Principal Swift's mouth, which at that moment contained exactly one barely eaten Gor-Monite breath mint.

"Gabby?" said a confused Swift. He'd given her explicit instructions: Jeremy was not to leave the house. "What are you—"

Gabby ran full force at Swift, lowering her shoulder into

his stomach. The mint he was sucking on flew from his mouth. Gabby followed the candy's trajectory as it arced through the air and across the cafeteria, nearing Jeremy. Jeremy's eyes grew wide. He stared at Gabby, who gave him an encouraging nod. He could do this. She believed in him.

Jeremy stepped back, leapt into the air, and opened wide. Bull's-eye! Jeremy threw his arms up in the air, victorious. "I did it!" he yelled. "I caught food in my mouth!"

"Yeah! You're not gonna die!" said Gabby, who'd run across the room to celebrate with him.

"That, too!" he said as an afterthought.

Gabby smiled as they high-fived. Why had she ever doubted herself? Who ruled at alien babysitting more than she did? So she almost blew up her Gor-Monite kid. But the important thing was that she didn't. All's great that ends great, right?

Principal Swift cleared his throat and scowled at them from across the room. Gabby noticed that Swift didn't look as happy as someone should when their nephew avoids total and complete explosion due to soda pop consumption. What was up with that?

⌐ ⌯ ⊤ △ ⋇ ⌂ ≏ ⊂ ⅍ ⊘

CHAPTER 9

"**W**hat you two did today was completely reck-less and could have easily resulted in Jeremy's explosion," Principal Swift said, glaring at Gabby and Jeremy across his office desk. He was clasping his hands together so tightly in anger that they were turning red.

Jeremy looked at his uncle. "But—"

Swift held up a hand, silencing him. "However, it did not," he continued. Swift's kind expression revealed that he'd been rather impressed with their high jinks. "And you did display remarkable poise and ingenuity in an emergency situation, which should probably count for something."

"So . . . am I fired?" Gabby asked, concern filling her voice.

Swift paused for what seemed like the single longest

moment of Gabby's young life. "Given the circumstances, I think it's fair to let you off with a stern warning this time—provided nothing like this ever happens again."

Yes! Gabby's face burst into the biggest smile ever. She was the most relieved she'd ever been. Before babysitting, she had nothing in Havensburg. No friends. No joy. No place she fit in. But babysitting aliens gave her purpose. She'd hit her stride. She looked at Jeremy, who was still squirming nervously in his seat.

"And you, Jeremy," snapped Swift, turning his attention toward his wayward nephew.

Jeremy sat up straight and braced himself for the worst. But it never came. Instead, Swift's mouth formed a small smirk. "That aerial attack was very convincing. If you could convince me you were one of those winged abominations, perhaps I've underestimated you."

Jeremy smiled. That was the first compliment he'd ever received from his uncle. Huh, maybe he could swing this Gor-Monite supreme-leader-in-training thing after all. Baller!

"And maybe to make up for that, you two could pick up some drive-through on the way home?" Gabby interjected.

She knew she should have stayed silent, but who was she kidding?

"Hmmmmmmmm. Fine. Why not?" said Swift, relenting. Secretly, he was quite curious about the primitive human habit of eating fastly prepared food while confined to one's personal mode of transportation. Of course, it made total sense, as it allowed the Earthlings to accomplish two critical things at once: fuel their bodies and give their car that highly coveted fresh french-fry scent. What would these creatures think of next?

"Baller!" shouted Jeremy, throwing in a fist pump.

Gabby had one more favor to ask of Swift. "Also, can I borrow some of your trash? I sort of did something to a friend of mine and need to make it up to him."

> 👽 <

When Wesley awoke, he found himself cramped inside the confines of the Havensburg Junior High janitor's closet. "Ugh . . . what happened?" he said, trying to shake off the grogginess.

Wesley froze. On the floor in front of him, someone had spelled out "Stop asking questions" in crumpled-up trash.

An enormous grin spread across his face. "I was right!"

He couldn't wait to tell the other Mysteries of Havensburg Club members—er, member—about this. He had to go find Gabby right away.

Standing in Gabby's room, Dina watched expectantly as Gabby studied the homemade Daughter of the Month certificate with her name on it. "What do you think?" asked Dina, proud of her DIY work. Using pink and yellow highlighters, she and Olivia had spent an hour getting the doodles just right. "I figure we can put it on the mantel downstairs."

"Daughter of the Month?" Gabby put her hand on her heart. "Mom, this is incredibly lame." And yet Gabby was quite touched by the gesture.

"I know, it's just Principal Swift told me what a great job you did babysitting for him," she said. "And I'm sorry I've been so hard on you lately. I know this whole moving thing hasn't been easy."

"Yeah, well, I suppose I probably could have handled things a little bit better," Gabby admitted.

"It's true," said Olivia, who'd been standing in the

doorway, listening. "But that's how we learn. I'm proud of your growth, Sis."

"Thanks, Liv." Gabby had to admit she was proud of her growth, too. She'd been trusted to guard the biggest secret in the universe, and she knew she could do it.

Dina suddenly remembered something. "Oh! And I also got you this," she said, handing Gabby a blue-and-yellow gift bag crammed with hot-pink tissue paper.

Gabby always enjoyed a good gift. She reached inside, excited to see what kind of unique present her mom had picked out for her. Gabby pulled out a Local 6 mug with Dina's picture on it.

"What? People love mugs," Dina said, laughing. Gabby laughed, too. She actually did kinda love that mug, because she loved her mom.

Just then, Gabby's cell phone chirped. Swift needed her.

Swift and Gabby walked together up the front steps of his house.

"Thank you for coming on such short notice," said Swift.

Gabby was happy to be back on the job. "That's what babysitting geniuses are for," she said, brushing off her shoulder with feigned modesty. "So what's up?"

Swift opened his front door to reveal a living room packed with alien families of all shapes and sizes, including a fish boy, a bald family with weird glowing lights on their heads, and what appeared to be a hamster-sized alien sitting inside a normal-sized android.

Gabby stopped in her tracks. "What the—"

A gray alien with oversized dark eyes waved at her, as if this was all perfectly normal.

Principal Swift explained, "Jeremy and I aren't the only aliens in need of babysitting help."

Gabby stared at the array of aliens. No way! It made sense that Swift and Jeremy weren't the only extraterrestrials living on Earth, but seeing them with her own two eyes was a whole different thing. She couldn't believe she had a super-awesome life-fulfilling babysitting gig. She couldn't believe the odor, either. "Wow," she said. "One of you smells real bad."

⌐⌐ ✂ ⊤ △ ⋇ ⌐ ≗ ⟙ ⅋ ∅

CHAPTER 10

Gabby and Wes stood together in the hallway waiting for the first-period bell to ring, just as they had every morning for the past few weeks. Gabby dug their daily routine. Nowadays, she was all about eyes to the future. Not only did she have a new best friend in Wes, but she had the most incredible new job in the world. Scratch that . . . in the galaxy.

Just the past week, she'd babysat for a multi-tentacled Zagellian baby who spit up blue goo and for fish boy Stewart, who hailed from the planet Vitreous Prime and had to wear a breathing device at all times. And, oh yeah, Wesley had uncovered her intergalactic secret. And for a paranormal conspiracy theorist like Wes, it didn't get more exciting than concrete proof of alien life. Gabby was glad to have someone to share her secret with. Being able to talk about everything with Wesley made life in Havensburg so much more fun.

At the moment, Wesley was standing in front of a row of red lockers, showing her a love-worn photo of a chocolate Labrador.

"Cool. A dog," said Gabby, whose outfit du jour was a cropped black-and-white checkerboard sweatshirt over a turquoise tee. She'd thrown on a green belt for accent.

"Not just a dog," Wesley corrected her, his voice cracking with emotion. "My dog, from when I was eight. His name was Brisket, and he loved belly rubs and broccoli. He was an original."

"I sense this story isn't going to end well," guessed Gabby, cocking her head to the side.

Wes shook his auburn head. "My parents took me out to ice cream one night and told me Brisket had died."

Gabby blanched. Losing someone you loved was never easy. "Oh, I'm sorry, bud."

Wesley cut her off. A new enthusiasm filled his voice.

"But I knew they were lying! He couldn't be dead. He was only fifteen years old! So I told myself he must've been abducted by aliens."

Gabby hesitated. She wasn't sure she liked where this conversation was going. "And now that you've met some aliens, you realize they don't need your dog and your parents were right?"

"No! I realize that it's totally possible he was abducted! And I'm gonna find him!" A look of determination came over his face as he slammed his locker shut and fastened the lock. "I'm coming for you, Brisket!" he shouted at full volume.

The students standing near Wes and Gabby all stopped and turned to look, curious about the cause of Wesley's outburst. Gabby threw her arm around Wes, taking him into her confidence. She had to put a stop to his alien talk—real fast.

As they walked down the hall, she gave him the low-down. "Listen, Wes, you gotta pump the brakes a bit," she said. "You're not supposed to know about any of this. I mean, look at me: I've known about the most incredible secret on Earth for weeks, and am I going around talking about alien dog abductions? No! All these kids know about me is that I'm the cool, tough new girl with the style that makes the kiddies go wild." Gabby broke into a self-congratulatory smile.

"Yeah, about that . . ." Wesley gestured toward a clique of kids who stood around their lockers, pointing and laughing. They sure seemed to be reacting to something hilarious.

"Who are they laughing at? You?" asked Gabby.

Wes shook his head. "Um . . . hurtful assumption, but fair." He really didn't want to deliver the soul-crushing news that she was the one being mocked. He shook his head and tried to lay it out gently. "Gabby, no. There's . . . kind of a rumor going around about you."

Gabby's brown eyes widened. A rumor? About her? What were they saying?

"So what's this rumor? It's probably something awesome, right? That I can do a standing backflip?" guessed Gabby.

"Kind of . . ." offered Wes. They stopped at Gabby's locker so she could stash her backpack before class. "They're saying you missed your old school so much you spent your first week here crying your eyes out in the girls' bathroom."

Gabby looked at him questioningly.

"Like snot-dripping-from-your-nose-into-your-mouth crying," he clarified, then wiggled his fingers to imitate a significant amount of snot flow.

"What?" Gabby said, shocked out of her socks. She stopped spinning her locker combo. "They said I was crying?"

"Yeah, everyone's calling you Crybaby Duran. Even the janitors."

Dobek the janitor suddenly leaned over Gabby's shoulder. How was he always popping up like that? Wesley was right: there was something suspicious about him. Dobek offered his two cents: "No shame in being weak."

Gabby glared at him. This couldn't be happening. Being called a crybaby was basically her worst nightmare. Next to the one when she woke up to find someone had stolen all her high-tops and she had to wear penny loafers to school. "Well, the joke's on them, 'cuz I don't cry. Like, ever. I didn't even cry when I was born. I came out like . . ." Gabby flexed her arms and struck a power stance.

Wes shook his head. "Come on, Gabby. Everybody cries. What's the big deal? I listened to an Adele album yesterday and bawled. She's been through so much," he said, getting teary-eyed just thinking about it.

Gabby put a consoling hand on Wes's shoulder. "Yeah, and that's fine." Then she switched tones completely. "But that's not me. I'm the tough girl. People say that: Gabby the tough girl."

"Do they?" Wes cocked his head.

"They're just a bunch of kids spreading a stupid rumor that's not even true!" Gabby said, raising her voice and whipping her hair around.

Gabby finished dialing her combination and opened her locker, which was in the top row. As she did, a tidal wave of tissues poured out.

Every student in the hallway cracked up at the cruel prank. Gabby did her best to act like it was no biggie. "Okay, good tissue burn, but I still don't care!" she shouted. Except, she did care. A lot.

CHAPTER 11

Gabby stared out the window of Principal Swift's office, her brain elsewhere. She'd thought meeting with Swift to discuss her next babysitting assignment would take her mind off her crybaby crisis, but the nickname was still top of mind.

"So her parents will be expecting you after school," concluded Swift with a smile.

There was no response from the normally energetic babysitter. Swift tapped on his desk. "Gabby, are you listening?"

Gabby snapped out of it. "Oh, yeah. Definitely."

Principal Swift remained unconvinced. The girl was clearly distracted, which was something he could not tolerate from someone with whom he'd entrusted such a big responsibility. "I was saying your babysitting assignment this afternoon is a telepathic alien named Sky."

That grabbed Gabby's attention. "Hmmmm, an alien who can read minds? That's dope," she said. She hadn't yet babysat an alien who possessed supernatural powers.

"Well, if 'dope' means her neural pathways align with anyone she touches, allowing her to download their thoughts and feelings into her brain, then yes. She's 'dope,'" agreed Swift, using air quotes.

Gabby cringed. If Swift wanted to seamlessly blend in with Earth culture, he'd have to stop with the air quotes. No normal human still used them.

Gabby's dinging cell phone interrupted her thought. She glanced at her phone, which she kept in a case that looked like an old cassette tape. "Uh, why is Jeremy texting me that you've locked him in the basement?" she asked.

Principal Swift seemed insulted by the very suggestion. "I haven't locked him anywhere. Jeremy is homeschooled while I'm at work. Can you imagine what would happen if Jeremy came to school?"

Gabby tried to picture it. She imagined Jeremy walking down the school hallway in human form, blending in no problem. He waved to kids at their lockers and high-fived friends. Then Jeremy felt a sneeze coming on. And everyone knew Gor-Mons couldn't hold their human shape and sneeze simultaneously. Just a weird blip in their biology. Jeremy instantly morphed into a giant blob in the middle of the hallway in front of everyone. A sudden sadness fell over Jeremy's face. "What's a blob gotta do to get a 'bless you' around here?" he asked, watching the students scream and scatter in a panic. His secret, and thus alien existence in Havensburg as a whole, was exposed. So, okay, yeah, having Jeremy at school would be a major problem.

"Got it," agreed Gabby emphatically. "No aliens at school."

"Anyway, don't worry about Jeremy," said Swift. "I'm sure he's completely engaged in his learning." Swift had made arrangements for the Orb to instill Jeremy with all the knowledge he'd need to someday rule their home planet.

In fact, at that precise moment, Jeremy was sitting behind the command desk in Swift's basement communications room, spinning aimlessly in his chair. He was most definitely not listening to the Orb, which floated in front of him, presenting a lecture on the geologic structure of Gor-Monia.

"The planet Gor-Monia is classified as a gassy giant.

When the gas within Gor-Monia's substrata heats, the pressure builds until the planet is in danger of exploding. As a result, Gor-Mons created a pressure-release matrix to ensure planetary stability," recited the Orb. Graphs and charts flashed on the three monitor screens that sat behind Jeremy's head.

Jeremy could not have looked less interested in the lesson.

"Pop quiz," challenged the Orb, its light blinking with a bit too much enthusiasm. It liked taunting Jeremy, whom the Orb felt had no business in the head honcho role. Still, the android did its best to fill the boy with knowledge. "What did the Gor-Mons create to ensure planetary stability?"

Jeremy stopped spinning in his chair long enough to answer the question. "Uh, my butt!" he said, laughing at his own joke.

"Heavy sigh," responded the Orb. Its panels flashed, and it buzzed with annoyance. Would this child ever be mature enough to rule?

As if in response, Jeremy launched a spitball through a straw and hit the Orb on its optical lens. Jeremy cracked himself up.

CHAPTER 12

Gabby's newest client, Sky, lived with her parents in a stark modern house on the edge of town. The chatty thirteen-year-old girl, who wore a high-necked maroon robe with oversized shoulder pads, had a bald head lined with thin glowing strands that lit up as she spoke to Gabby.

"So yeah, I'm really into teen stuff," Sky explained. Even though she'd never met an Earthling teen before, she was obsessed. She'd binge-watched all movies, series, and online clips she could find about the dramatic ups and downs of teenage life. She'd made dream boards for her walls, all featuring photo collages of hunky teenage heart-throbs with smoldering expressions and teen girl squads in semiformal dresses. A clear plastic chair with a sequined crown-shaped pillow sat in the corner. Sky had read that teens loved anything with a little bling.

"Wow. I see that," said Gabby, eyeing Sky's posters that weirdly celebrated the generic topics of music, teens, and prom.

"Meeting a teen is so exciting!" exclaimed Sky. She pulled up a hot-pink vinyl chair so she could sit as close as possible to Gabby. Having been cooped up in her parents' house since their arrival on Earth, Sky craved social interaction with others her age.

"What's up with the old guy?" asked Gabby, pointing to a cardboard cutout of a middle-aged man wearing a large Elizabethan collar and red cape. The dude was definitely out of place among Sky's cool teen decor.

"It's Drake," Sky said, swooning.

Gabby looked at her, totally perplexed. She was going to need a bit more information.

"Sir Francis Drake? Famed English privateer? Teens love Drake, right?" bubbled Sky.

"Um, not that Drake." Gabby explained. Sky still had a lot to learn, but hey, that's why her parents hired a sitter, Gabby figured.

"So, question," said Gabby, putting her hands in her lap. "If you're thirteen and I'm thirteen, why am I babysitting

69

you? I haven't had a babysitter since I was nine."

Sky, too, thought the arrangement was odd. "I don't think my parents get what babysitters are," she said. "Probably because the word *babysitter* sounds a lot like our word *babasata*, which means 'one who teaches math.'"

"Hmmm, that would explain why he gave me this." Gabby held up a calculator. She'd assumed Sky's dad presented it as part of some strange customary alien greeting.

Just then, Sky's dad entered the bedroom. He was a tall man whose bald head was marked with the same lit-up lines as his daughter's. Gabby found his ultra-zen aura unnerving. "Salutations, Gabby. Sky's mother and I leave now. You have good babysitting."

Gabby punched some keys on the calculator and smiled. Why bother explaining? She'd sat for enough aliens to know sometimes it wasn't worth trying to explain things to them.

Mr. Sky's Dad crossed to his daughter and, closing his eyes, touched his forehead to hers. The lights on their heads blinked in sync. After a moment, he opened his eyes, gave his daughter a smile of understanding, and went on his way.

"So . . . you guys don't speak?" Gabby asked Sky once her dad had shut the door.

"Not really. When you're a telepath, it's just quicker that way," she explained. "I need you to tell me everything about what it's like to be a teen girl," she told Gabby.

Gabby wasn't sure where to start. There was so much to teen life on Earth: juggling the pressures of friendships, family, homework, and fashion. It wasn't always easy. Gabby's mind wandered to her new nickname. She grimaced at the thought. "I hate to break it to you," said Gabby, looking down at her purple-painted nails, "but being a teenager here isn't all that great."

"It's not? Why?" Sky's face filled with disappointment. The only thing she'd ever dreamed about was becoming an Earthling teen.

"Doesn't matter," Gabby said, then quickly changed the subject. "I wanna see this mind reading in action." She held out her arm for Sky. As a touch telepath, Sky could only read the thoughts of a person with whom she shared physical contact. Sky wrapped both her hands around Gabby's forearm, then closed her eyes to deepen the connection.

A moment passed.

"So what was I thinking?" inquired Gabby, eager to see the superpower work firsthand.

"You were wondering if eating toothpaste and just swishing it around in your mouth is the same as brushing your teeth," said Sky, releasing Gabby's arm.

"I think it might be!" said Gabby, impressed. That had been a very private oral hygiene theory.

A look of concern fell across Sky's pale blue eyes. She'd sensed more in Gabby's mind. "But you were also thinking about something else. Something that's bothering you."

"What are you talking about? Nothing bothers me," said Gabby, brushing it off.

Sky considered Gabby for a beat. While Gabby spoke of being tough, her thoughts had signaled otherwise. Perhaps Sky should take a second look. "Hey! Look over there!" shouted Sky, pointing at nothing in particular across the room. When Gabby turned to look, Sky reached out and touched her arm again. The lights on Sky's head flickered as she received the telepathic transmission.

"Hey!" said Gabby, jumping up in surprise. "That is a terrible invasion of privacy!"

But the process was already in motion. Sky appraised Gabby's thoughts with a mix of confusion and empathy. "Kids at school call you Crybaby Duran. And you hate it."

"Of course I hate it!" said Gabby. Her tone was slightly defensive. "If people see me as the kid who cries in the bathroom, they won't realize I'm actually the cool, hip girl they can't help but love!" That was how Gabby hoped that everyone in Havensburg would come to see her.

Gabby's phone buzzed in her pocket. She pulled it out to find Wes video-calling from Luchachos, their favorite taqueria in town.

"Bad news," said Wes before Gabby could even squeeze in a hello. "So the Crybaby Duran thing that was definitely gonna blow over? It's kind of a dance now."

Wes angled his phone so Gabby could see a group of giggling girls performing the Crybaby Duran dance. The dance seamlessly married flossing with a brand-new move: pantomiming waa-waa eyes. Gabby had to admit the choreography was annoyingly catchy.

She put the phone down and turned to Sky. "You see what I'm dealing with here?" Middle school was supposed to be about Gabby blowing the minds of her fellow students with her hip dance moves and ultracool vibes. Instead, she was battling a widespread rumor about her being a sobbing Sally. The situation was out of control.

"So what are you going to do?" asked Sky. Having never attended a human school or been the subject of hurtful teen ridicule, Sky was unclear if a solution existed for such a problem.

"I don't know what I can do," said Gabby, shaking her head in frustration. "It's not like I can just find out who started the rumor and make them take it back. I'm not a mind reader."

Hold up! Gabby shot Sky a mischievous look. Sky nodded in total agreement. "I don't even have to touch you to know what you're thinking. And yes, I'm in." Sky couldn't wait to be part of a real-life teenage adventure.

"Good. 'Cuz tomorrow, you and I have some minds to read." Gabby grinned.

⌐ ⊁ ⊤ △ ⅄ ⅃ ≌ ⌐ ⌐ ⑂ ⊘

CHAPTER 13

*T**he next morning, Gabby was up before her alarm**
even went off. She planned to put a stop to that crybaby
rumor with one fun-filled day of alien telepathy.

Gabby climbed through Sky's bedroom window, fired
up to get the party started. "All right, who's ready for
schooooool?" cried Gabby, tripping over the Sir Francis
Drake cardboard cutout.

"Sorry, fake Drake," Gabby said, standing the explorer
back up. That was when she noticed Sky, in the exact same
outfit she had worn the day before.

"Okay, first things first," said Gabby. "I love this look,
but I don't think junior high is ready for it yet. Maybe we
can add a hat? Burn that robe?" Floor-length robes might
fly with Supreme Court justices and college graduates, but
the style had yet to trickle down to middle schoolers.

"I collect teen memorabilia. Will that help?" asked Sky, opening the doors to her closet.

Gabby eyed the racks of hip clothes and cool accessories with a smile. A makeover session, like one of those montages from a classic teen film, was definitely in order. Sky was about to live her teen-girl dream, and she needed to look the part.

Since Sky's glowing scalp would stick out in the school hallway, Gabby started by grabbing a stack of hats from the shelves. She tried a metallic silver cap, a pale pink beret, and a multicolored bucket hat, none of which worked with Sky's bald head. Gabby suggested a green cowboy hat and a sequined painter's cap before reaching for a shoulder-length blond wig.

"That'll work," confirmed Gabby. The light color looked natural against Sky's pale skin. This alien could really rock the long-layers look.

Sky stared at her reflection in the mirror, stunned. "I look like a cool teen!"

Next Gabby swiped tinted lip gloss across Sky's mouth, then grabbed a tube of mascara. "I've actually never put mascara on another person before," she said. "How poke-resistant are your eyes?" From Sky's expression, Gabby could tell the answer was "not very."

Then Sky stepped into her closet and came out modeling a black jumper, a beige turtleneck, and a pair of oversized glasses. "You look like my aunt Harriet," said Gabby, frowning. Not that there was anything wrong with her favorite tia, but Aunt Harriet was pushing seventy-eight.

Next Sky selected a striped sweater and a pair of pink overalls, with only one shoulder fastened. "I like it," cheered Sky, a fan of that look.

"Me too," said Gabby, staring down at her own striped-sweater-and-one-shouldered-overall combo. "But I don't do twins."

For her final first-day-of-school look, Sky paired gray skinny jeans with an ocean-blue sweater and a dark denim jacket.

"Bingo! The perfect middle school look," declared Gabby. "A little bit geek and a little bit chic."

"I feel dope to the max," gushed Sky.

Gabby laughed. "We'll work on the lingo," she said. It

wasn't even nine a.m. and she was already having a fun day.

Just then, Wesley appeared in Sky's window. Like Gabby, he crashed into the cardboard cutout as he climbed through. "Sorry, Sir Francis Drake," said Wesley. "I love that guy!"

Gabby helped Wesley and the famed explorer back to their feet. "And sorry I'm late," Wes said. "My dad wasn't buying my usual sick routine. I had to actually throw up."

Gabby and Sky exchanged awkward looks, unsure what to say about Wes's extra effort. Gabby decided it was a statement for which there was no appropriate comeback, so she skipped straight to the introductions. "Wesley, this is Sky. Sky, Wesley."

Wesley reached out and shook Sky's hand, thrilled to be in the presence of a certified extraterrestrial. "Super excited to meet you. So, what am I thinking?"

"You're super excited to meet me," said Sky, reading his mind. "And you miss your dog, Brisket?"

Wesley's mouth turned down at the corners, and his eyes filled with tears. "That dog was a brother to me."

"Okay, people," Gabby said, seamlessly taking on the

leadership role, "Sky told her very gullible parents she was gonna sleep all day. Wes, that's where you come in. You'll stay here and pretend to be her. We're counting on you. If Sky's dad finds out Sky's missing, we're toast."

Wesley nodded. Lucky for Sky, he took his alien interactions very seriously. He'd practically spent his whole life training for this moment. Besides, how dangerous could her dad really be?

"If my dad does catch you, and the lights on his head turn red, you should run. Like, ruuuuuuun," said Sky.

"Okay, then!" said Gabby, patting Wes on the back. "No backing out now! See ya!"

"Yeah!" chimed in Sky, waving cheerfully.

Gabby grabbed Sky and led her out the window. They had a rumor to stop.

⌐ ✕ ⊤ △ ✕ ⌐ ≡ �5 ℅ ⊘

CHAPTER 14

*E*arthling teen life was everything Sky had imagined and more. Walking down the Havensburg Junior High hall, Sky wasn't sure where to look first. Everything was so cool: kids with backpacks, sporting sneakers and carrying reusable water bottles. "So this is junior high," she said, gawking. "Look! Lockers!" Her mouth fell open as she gaped at the red lockers that lined every wall.

Gabby was amused by Sky's amazement. There was something charming and refreshing about it.

"Is that a jock?" asked Sky, having read all about them in her teen romance novels. She was positive the boy at his locker a few feet away was one of them.

"I'll school you on school later," said Gabby, pretty sure the bookish boy in the fleece hadn't kicked or thrown a ball around in his life. "Let's find out who started this rumor before Swift spots us, since I'm not supposed to bring aliens to school."

Sky sprinted up to the maybe jock and placed both her hands on his cheeks. She couldn't wait to read his thoughts.

"Whoa, whoa, whoa," said Gabby, pulling Sky away from the startled boy. "We don't touch other kids' faces like that in middle school. Or anywhere else, really."

"Oh, sorry," Sky said.

Gabby threw her arm around Sky and leaned in con- spiratorially. "What you want to do is accidentally bump into someone on purpose, like this." Gabby gently shoved Sky right into a girl wearing glasses.

The girl brushed it off, assuming Sky was just some kind of klutz. But the brief encounter was enough to allow Sky to read her mind.

"Get anything?" asked Gabby, eager to discover who had started the rumor about her.

"She picked her nose twenty minutes ago and is trying to figure out where to put it."

Gabby made a gagging face. "Good to know. She sits behind me in math class." She made a mental note to scoot her chair forward a bit in fourth period.

Sky buzzed down the hall in glee, the silver mini backpack Gabby had picked out for her bouncing with every step. As Sky walked by the bathroom, she noticed a handmade sign taped to the door. "'Crybaby Duran's House,'" read Sky. "That's bad, right?" Beneath the words, someone had drawn a sad face.

"Yeah, it's bad," said Gabby, ripping the sign down and crumpling it into a ball. "For whoever started this rumor." Nobody called Gabby Duran a crybaby and got away with it. "Now, let's—"

Gabby lost her train of thought as she saw Principal Swift walking down the hall straight toward them. If he caught Sky at school, Gabby's alien babysitting days were over. And Gabby was not about to let that happen. There was only one solution: Gabby shoved Sky into the janitor's closet.

"Wha—" Sky yelped in protest. But Gabby slammed the door before Sky could finish her thought.

As she did, Swift, all gangly legs and awkward arms,

strode up to her. "So, Gabby. I trust everything went well at Sky's house yesterday."

Never great at lying, Gabby began to ramble. "Yep, sure did. She's definitely not here. She's at home. Not here at school, because that would be against the rules." She glanced sideways at the janitor's closet. "She's not here."

"Carry on, then." Swift nodded, oblivious.

Gabby realized one good thing about having an alien for a principal was that he was slow to sense when something was amiss. Everything Earthling teens did seemed strange to him, so why would Gabby's odd behavior stand out? With Swift out of sight, Gabby pulled Sky from the closet, hoping she wasn't too traumatized.

She wasn't. "I found a new wig!" she announced, wearing a mop on her head. She parted the strings to frame her face, then tucked a few ropes behind her ears.

"Cool!" Gabby smiled, immediately removing the mop from Sky's head and tossing it back in the closet. She so badly wanted to teach Sky what was and wasn't considered cool in junior high, but first they had a crybaby quest to complete.

Deep in the basement of Principal Swift's house, the floating Orb continued to lecture Jeremy on the finer points of Gor-Monite geology. As it spoke, its pentagon-shaped panels moved in and out, in sync with its speech pattern. "To understand the intricacies of the pressure-release matrix, we must—"

"*Buuuuuurrrrrrp.*" Jeremy belched. He was beyond bored with the tedious lesson.

The Orb clicked and chirped, then extended its laser scalpel toward Jeremy's head. "Enough is enough. You will learn," demanded the Orb.

Jeremy stared at the Orb, unfazed and unintimidated. "Sorry, Orb. No one makes me learn." He morphed into his green blob form, opened his mouth wide, and roared at the Orb through his gaping maw. The Orb backpedaled. Perhaps it would try a new approach to its lesson plan.

Meanwhile, Wesley was spending his sick day checking out Sky's teen paraphernalia collection. As president of the Mysteries of Havensburg Club, Wes found it fascinating to see life on Earth through an alien's eyes. Plus, he was wigging out just thinking about the fact that he was sitting in an actual extraterrestrial's room.

"Sky," called Sky's dad, knocking on the door.

Wes tried not to panic, but on the other side of that knock was a full-grown adult alien whom he'd been warned not to anger. He'd read enough sci-fi books to know that good things never came from angering aliens. Thinking quickly, he jumped into the bed and hid under the fuzzy pink covers. Sky's dad opened the door and moved toward the bed. The lights on his head flashed as he leaned down to speak to his daughter telepathically.

"Wait!" cried Wes, speaking in a terrible high-pitched imitation of a girl's voice. He had to stop Sky's dad from pulling back the covers. "I mean . . . may we practice speaking human?" For some reason, Wesley's awful girl voice also involved a cockney accent. He really hoped Sky's dad was buying it.

Sky's dad leaned back from the bed, puzzled. Sky sounded strange. "Your talking voice is odd to me—I hear it not much, I suppose. Very well." He stood back up and walked toward the door. "I brought the man's best friend for keeping company." He let a fluffy chocolate Labrador into the room, then left and closed the door.

Wesley pulled the covers off his head. He sat up, stunned at the sight before him. There, in Sky's room, was . . . could it be? "No way! Brisket?" asked Wes tentatively.

The dog wagged his tail and tilted his head as if he recognized his name. Then he sat obediently and stared up at Wesley with his irresistible giant puppy-dog eyes.

⊓ ⋊ ⊤ △ ⋎ ⊡ ≗ �5 ⅋ ∅

CHAPTER 15

Gabby and Sky were laughing as they rounded the corner. Sky had an openness and enthusiasm about her that Gabby enjoyed. As they made their way down the hall, Gabby spotted a curly-haired girl scrolling through her phone in front of her locker. "Okay, there's Molly," Gabby told Sky. "She's the biggest gossip in school. I guarantee you she knows something. Go get her."

Gabby hung back and waited expectantly as Sky walked toward Molly. She accidentally-on-purpose brushed up against Molly's gray sweater sleeve, just as Gabby had demonstrated. She returned to Gabby with a giant grin.

"So? What'd you discover?" asked Gabby, waiting for the big reveal.

Sky took a deep breath, then dove in at rapid-fire speed.

"Molly heard the rumor from Ted, who likes her, but she totes has a crush on Isaac, but he likes Jenna, so she can't even! Crazy, right? Oh, snap, we should go find Isaac!"

Okay, that was way too much information. "I think you're getting a little too into the teen drama," said Gabby. "I don't need to know everything that's going on with everyone in school. I just need to know who started the rumor about me. Focus."

Sky took a step back. "Focus? Focus on what? On this Jenna girl everyone's thinking about? What's so special about her? I know, right?"

Gabby looked at Sky, who was clearly overwhelmed. She gently put her hand on Sky's arm. "Yeah, maybe it wasn't such a great idea bringing you here," she said. "I think I should take you home."

"What?" roared Sky. "Home? No way! I wanna find out more!" Sky was finally living her dream. She was interacting with other beings her age, and she was not about to give that up. Not even for her new friend, Gabby. Sky bolted down the hall, sprinting away from Gabby as quickly as she could. "I love teen stuff! Whoooooo!" she shouted, brushing up against as many students as possible and reading their gossip-filled minds.

Back at Sky's house, Wesley sat on the corner of the bed, comparing his dog-eared picture of Brisket to the panting dog before him. They looked exactly the same. Wesley knew he had to test his hypothesis.

"Speak," he instructed. The dog barked.

"High-five," he commanded. The dog placed his adorable paw atop Wesley's hand.

"Fetch," directed Wesley, picking up Sky's pink beret and tossing it across the room. The dog didn't move. Wesley nodded in appreciation. "Brisket was always too proud to fetch."

The dog thumped his tail in agreement.

All signs pointed to yes, this had to be Brisket. Wes reasoned that if aliens could be living down the street in Havensburg, it wasn't too far-fetched that his old dog could be living under one of their roofs. "There's only one sure way to know if you're my dog, though," said Wes. "We need broccoli."

When Wes was eight years old, he hated broccoli. Every night, his mom would make it for dinner. And every night at dinner, Wes would feed it to Brisket under the table. Wes couldn't understand why, but his dog loved the vegetable. He couldn't get enough of it. So Wes reasoned that if Sky's dog was also a huge fan of broccoli, he had to be Brisket.

Wes opened the bedroom door and silently snuck down the hall. He passed the den, where Sky's dad was meditating in a podlike recliner with his eyes closed. Careful not to disturb him, Wes tiptoed the rest of the way to the kitchen.

The kitchen was modern and sparse, like the rest of the house. Wes opened the stainless steel refrigerator to discover a definitive lack of broccoli. In fact, shelf after shelf was filled with stacked cans of green beans. He shut the fridge and opened the cabinets only to see the same. Wes tried another cabinet, but it was no different. "Green beans! So close!" muttered Wes in frustration.

Wes heard the den door close; Sky's dad was on the move. No sooner had Wes slid down behind the kitchen counter than Sky's dad walked into the room. The alien picked up a lone white mug from the counter and placed it in the sink. He noticed a cabinet door was open. He looked around suspiciously, then closed it before walking out. Wes remained crouched behind the counter for a few more minutes, frozen in fear.

Meanwhile, Gabby was dealing with her own alien crisis. She'd searched all over the school but hadn't located Sky. She turned a corner near the science wing and finally spotted her. "Sky, there you are!"

Sky was fired up. "Gabby, I just heard the coolest thing! Do you know there's also a rapper named Drake?"

"We gotta get you home," suggested Gabby.

"I told you, I can't go home! Not when there's so much teen knowledge to absorb!" Sky spread her arms out wide and spun.

Just then, the school bell rang and throngs of students flooded out of the classrooms and into the hall. Tall kids, short kids, punk kids, emo kids—all jostling Sky as they passed her on the way to their next classes. Gabby got separated from Sky and watched helplessly as Sky bounced from student to student like a blond pinball. Bumping into kids from every angle, Sky absorbed an astronomical bar-rage of brain waves. "Test next period. I have to go to the library. Where is Lisa? She said she'd meet me. . . ." Sky started to tremble as she repeated the semi-coherent thought fragments she'd picked up from the students. "I love Manny. Dancing. School dance. Class. Teacher. Gym. Headbands. Should I grow a mustache?" Sky's head lolled as she glitched and sputtered nonsense.

Freaking out, Gabby pulled her friend from the depths of the crowd and led her to the principal's office. Admitting she'd screwed up, especially to Principal Swift, was not high on her bucket list, but she had no choice. She had to put Sky's safety first. It was what any good babysitter would do.

Gabby burst into Swift's office with Sky in tow. He took one look at the girls and his face contorted into bewilder-ment. "Oh, Gabby. What on Earth?" he asked, standing up behind his desk.

Sky was muttering incoherently. "Hairy legs. No one likes me. I miss you, Nana."

Gabby's eyes pleaded with Swift; she was desperate for help. "I broke Sky."

⌐◻ ✕ ⊤ △ ⫟ ◪ ≗ ꘓ ℅ ∅

CHAPTER 16

Swift and Gabby darted into the comms room, where blob Jeremy and the Orb were circling each other in a face-off.

"You can't make me learn," snapped Jeremy, his giant mouth wide open.

The Orb swiped at the blob with its laser scalpel. "Care to test that theory?" it threatened.

"Nice try!" shouted Jeremy triumphantly. "Tests and theories are both learning!"

Gabby stared at the unlikely sparring partners. "What is going on?"

Swift, who held the rambling Sky in his arms, had greater tasks to attend to. He brushed by the bickering duo. "Don't mind them. This happens literally every day. Jeremy! Orb! Cease at once."

Jeremy morphed back into human form. The Orb retracted its scalpel with a whirl. "Sorry," it said to Jeremy, who cocked his head inquisitively when he noticed Sky sputtering.

"I hate math. Jockstraps. Grounded for life," she muttered as her head swiveled back and forth.

Swift set Sky in the command console chair and removed her stylish wig. The lights on her head flashed with irregularity, switching between red and green at random.

"Whoa. Cool . . ." said Jeremy, enjoying the light show.

"No, not cool, Jeremy," corrected Swift. He turned to Gabby, his lips forming an angry line. "This is why we don't bring aliens to school."

Gabby felt awful as she watched Sky's spasms. "I know, I get it! But we have to help her. What can we do?"

"Our Orb is programmed with medical procedures for a variety of life-forms," Swift informed her. He turned to the Orb with specific instructions. "Initiate synaptic clearance protocol."

A medical apparatus popped out of one of the Orb's panels and emitted a red energy-beam scan.

"Mind scan initiated," reported the Orb. The moment the beam hit Sky's forehead, she froze in place. Not even a blink. For the first time since the hallway incident, Sky went silent.

Gabby, Swift, and Jeremy watched with anxious anticipation as the scan attempted to relieve Sky's overcrowded telepathic receptors. The Orb disengaged its probe and floated backward. "Protocol failure. Too many synaptic pathways to clear."

Sky's friends were overcome with the gut punch of disappointment and defeat. Swift threw up his arms, frustrated by his inability to help the young girl. Gabby brought her hand to her forehead in disbelief. There had to be a way to save Sky.

Sky's rambling continued to accelerate. "Friends. Rainbows. Tests. Fairies."

Gabby looked down at her shoes, her heart heavy with shame. "This is all my fault. The bell rang and all those kids banged into her—it's like there were too many thoughts and the pressure got too much."

"The pressure is too much," said Jeremy, trying to recall why that sounded familiar. His eyes shone with a look of realization. He knew this one! "You need somewhere for all those thoughts to go! Like some sort of pressure-release matrix!"

Swift and Gabby stared at Jeremy, amazed. His idea was genius.

"Jeremy, that's it!" said Swift, his face lighting up like a spaceship at takeoff. Not only did they have a solution, but the brilliant notion had come from none other than his nephew. He couldn't have been prouder.

"Orb, download Sky's thoughts and emotions into your digital matrix," instructed Swift. He'd never felt so relieved.

"Not possible," answered the Orb. "My neural core cannot absorb human brain patterns. We require a human host."

All eyes turned to Gabby. "What?" she asked, not liking the way Swift and Jeremy were looking at her.

CHAPTER 17

The Chow Down delivery guy thought it had been an odd request and rechecked the special instructions. Yup, it definitely said to bring the food directly to the first-floor bedroom window. Do not stop at the front door. Do not ring the bell. The good news was special instructions usually resulted in a nice fat tip. He rubbed his hands on his navy vest, then knocked on the window and held up the brown paper bag. "Steamed broccoli for Brisket?"

"Yep, thanks," said Wesley, grabbing the food and turning away.

The delivery guy waited a beat, but nothing happened. "Lemme guess. No tip?"

"How about a tip of the cap?" suggested Wesley, tipping an imaginary cap on his head.

The delivery guy was about to express his displeasure when someone knocked on the bedroom door. Wesley pushed the delivery guy away and scrambled to shut the curtains.

"Sky?" called Sky's dad from the other side of the door.

Wesley raised his voice two octaves, trying to sound like Sky. "One second! Don't come in!" he sang.

"I heard strange sounds," said Sky's dad. "Is it danger?" The lights on his head started to glow a menacing red.

Wesley grasped for an answer. "That was me!" he responded in his girly voice. Then he switched to his normal, lower voice. "I'm practicing my male Earthling voice." He knew as soon as he'd said it that it was a lame excuse. Sky's dad would never buy it.

"That is quite silly!" her dad responded, the red pulsing lights on his head subsiding. "But it does not sound real. Continue practice."

Phew, that had been close. But for Wesley, when it came to Brisket, no risk was too high. Wesley turned his attention to the dog, who sat waiting obediently. The dog's tail wagged back and forth with excitement as Wesley kneeled next to him on the floor.

Wesley scratched the dog's ears, then opened the take-out container and set it in front of the pup. "Go ahead, boy. Eat." Wesley knew Brisket would leap at the sight of the big box of broccoli.

But the dog stared at the food, uninterested.

"It's your favorite," Wesley reminded him. "Come on. Like this." Wesley lowered his head to the box and ate the broccoli straight out of it like a dog.

Unimpressed, Brisket set his head down on the floor. Wesley studied the canine. It was the same eyes, the same light patch on the ears, and the same happy tail. And yet something was off. "Brisket would never turn this down," Wesley said sadly. "You're not Brisket, are you, boy?"

The dog rolled onto his back. Wesley scratched his tummy lovingly. Then Wesley noticed: "Plus, you're a girl!"

CHAPTER 18

*J*eremy and Swift positioned Gabby and Sky in side-by-side chairs. The Orb zipped around in front of them, its medical beam device at the ready.

"Gabby, are you sure you want to proceed with the thought transfer into your brain?" asked Principal Swift. Gabby's actions were commendable, but he felt obligated to remind her of the risks. "It may relieve the pressure on Sky, but there's no telling what might happen to you."

Gabby looked over at Sky, who was still mumbling nonsense. "School. Happy. Homework. Gym class."

There was a chance Gabby would end up in the same state. But what kind of future did she have if she had to spend it knowing she'd ruined Sky? Gabby shuddered. Nope, there was no question about it. "I got Sky into this mess. I'm getting her out of it." Besides, she told herself, if there was one thing Gabby Duran was, it was tough. She could handle this brain-transfer thingy no problem, right?

Principal Swift smiled, proud of Gabby's choice. What a special teen she was. Once again, she reminded him why, of all the humans he'd met in Havensburg, he'd entrusted Gabby to babysit the unsittables.

Gabby looked over at Sky. The lights on her head pulsed rapidly as she continued to mumble. Gabby reached out bravely and grabbed hold of Sky's hand. The probe activated, sending dual beams of pulsing energy into each of the girls' foreheads. The beams crackled and snapped as they penetrated the teens' brains, causing both subjects to freeze. Within moments, Gabby was reading all the thoughts Sky had collected from students earlier that day:

I love Ted. I've got to steal his sweater so I can smell him.

I haven't brushed my teeth in days. Does my breath smell?

Crybaby Duran has cool sneakers.

I hate football. I just want to dance.

Did she really cry for a whole week?

The thoughts of Havensburg Junior High's population kept coming at Gabby, faster and faster. Gabby's brain whirled as the students' fears and concerns swirled through her neural pathways.

How could I fail science?

I have fat ankles.

Do people like my backpack?

Nana's never coming back.

Finally, the floating Orb halted the blazing energy beams and withdrew its medical device. "Thought transfer complete."

Swift and Jeremy ran to Sky's side as she opened her eyes. The lights on her head had returned to normal. She looked around the room with a refreshed smile on her face, as if she'd just awoken from the most delicious nap. "Hi, everyone. What's going on?"

Swift clasped his hands together in front of his chest. "Thank goodness. Now I don't have to write a lengthy apology to Sky's parents," he said. But it was clear from his overjoyed expression that he was grateful for much more than that.

"Oooooh, Gabby, how are you?" Swift asked.

In contrast to Sky's cheerful demeanor, Gabby was bawling her eyes out. Tears streamed down her face uncontrollably and her voice caught in her throat. "Jessica thinks she has fat ankles. That's why she wears tube socks. And Isaac likes Samantha, but she doesn't like him back. And there are so many grandmas who died," she sobbed.

Sky put her hand on Gabby's arm, hoping to bring comfort to her friend. Swift reached into his pants pocket and retrieved a silk handkerchief. Always the gentleman, he handed it to Gabby.

Gabby dabbed at her eyes. "I guess I am Crybaby Duran after all." She blew her nose so loudly she jumped at the noise.

She considered all she'd discovered during the thought transfer. "The sad thing is, all anyone was thinking about is what other people were thinking about them. So if you think about it, it doesn't make sense to worry about what other people think about you because all those people are thinking about is what other people are thinking about them."

Principal Swift and Jeremy stared at her, both wearing

blank expressions. "I didn't understand any of that," admitted Swift. He hadn't pegged Gabby for the philosophical type. That girl was just full of surprises. "But I'm glad everyone's okay."

Sky looked at Gabby with newfound respect. "Gabby, you deal with all those crazy thoughts and gossip and rumors every day?"

"Pretty much."

Sky nodded in admiration. "Wow, being a teen girl is harder than I thought!"

"Tell me about it," Gabby said. She had always thought she was the only one struggling at school. She hadn't realized until that day just how hard it was for everyone else. "We still didn't find out who started the whole Crybaby Duran thing."

"Oh, yes. Ha-ha. Oh, that was me," said Swift, raising his finger in the air, full of false modesty.

Gabby and Sky stood up from their chairs simultaneously.

"Why would you do that?" gasped Sky.

Swift turned to Gabby. "You've been such a big help to

me these past few weeks that I wanted to return the favor in kind." He appeared quite pleased with himself for thinking up such a clever plan.

Gabby's mouth fell open in shock. "By telling everyone I cried like a baby?"

"Yes, well, humans seem to adore their babies, so I assumed if I told people that you cried like one, everyone would think you were dope to the max."

Gabby wanted to be mad at Swift's baffling actions, but she couldn't help smiling. "That's actually kinda sweet. But please don't ever try to help me like that again."

ᒣ ✂ ⊤ △ ☒ ᒪ ≗ ⌐ ⅌ ⦸

CHAPTER 19

Sky and Gabby quickly returned to Sky's house. They'd been gone much longer than intended, and the chances of them not getting caught sneaking back in were rather slim. They scrambled through Sky's bedroom window, where they found Wesley sitting on the bed, waiting.

He popped up when he saw them. "Where've you guys been? Sky's dad has checked in on me ten times," he said. "That guy gives you no space."

"Long story," said Gabby. She'd fill Wesley in on all the details later. She put her hand on Sky's shoulder. "Listen, Sky, I'm really sorry for short-circuiting your brain today."

"Are you kidding?" gushed Sky. "I got to go to school, dress like a teenager, and do gossip. Aside from almost dying, it was the greatest day of my life!" Her eyes danced with glee.

"That's actually pretty typical for a day with Gabby," confirmed Wesley. His life had improved massively since Gabby got to town.

"You think you'd wanna hang out again sometime?" Sky asked. "But, you know, not as a babysitter. If you want to. I mean, we're friends, right?"

Lucky for Sky, Gabby Duran took her friendships very seriously. "Sky, c'mon. After what we just went through, we'd better be!" In truth, it was Gabby who felt lucky to have made a new friend as amazing as Sky. Something told her they had a lot of adventures ahead of them.

After saying good-bye to Sky, Gabby realized she was starving. She and Wesley grabbed their usual booth at Luchachos Taqueria. The restaurant had sombreros on the wall, Mexican wrestlers in the logo, and the best quesadillas in town. Maybe the state.

"Sorry Sky's dog wasn't your dog," said Gabby, her arms folded on top of the table.

"Yeah, me too." Wes nodded. "I guess I just have to face the fact that Brisket's gone and he's never coming back." He shrugged with reluctant acceptance.

As Gabby reached for a sip of water, the waitress

brought their order: one large quesadilla. Wesley stared at the food in front of him, his eyes wide with wonder.

"What?" asked Gabby, her eyes also wide but with hunger.

"The quesadilla! It's Brisket! It's his face!" said Wesley, spinning the plate so Gabby could see for herself.

Sure enough, the quesadilla had an image of a dog's face burned into the tortilla.

"Gabby, this is a sign," Wesley said, all fired up. He gestured wildly at the miracle quesadilla. "Brisket's still alive. And I'm never going to stop looking for him. And when I find him, I'm—"

Wesley stopped midsentence, his eyes burning into Gabby as she took a huge bite out of a quesadilla wedge. The melted cheese strung from her mouth. "Sorry, I was hungry," she said with her mouth full. "It's been a long day." Besides, the best babysitter in the galaxy deserved the best quesadilla in the galaxy—mysterious dog face or not.

Gabby looked across the booth at Wesley, thrilled to have found such a fun and loyal best friend in her new town. Between that and her intergalactic babysitting gig, Gabby had to admit her life in Havensburg was pretty dope.